Callie
the Climbing
Fairy

Join the **Rainbow Magic Reading Challenge!**

Read the story and collect your fairy points to climb the

To Lara Christina, who loves climbing

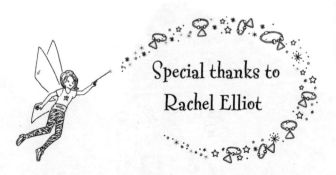

Special thanks to
Rachel Elliot

ORCHARD BOOKS

First published in Great Britain in 2019 by The Watts Publishing Group

1 3 5 7 9 10 8 6 4 2

© 2019 Rainbow Magic Limited.
© 2019 HIT Entertainment Limited.
Illustrations © Orchard Books 2019

HIT entertainment

A CIP catalogue record for this book is available from the British Library.

ISBN 978 1 40835 526 8

Printed and bound in Great Britain by Clays Ltd, Elcograf S.p.A.

MIX
Paper from
responsible sources
FSC® C104740

The paper and board used in this book are made from wood from responsible sources

Orchard Books
An imprint of Hachette Children's Group
Part of The Watts Publishing Group Limited
Carmelite House, 50 Victoria Embankment, London EC4Y 0DZ

An Hachette UK Company
www.hachette.co.uk
www.hachettechildrens.co.uk

Callie
the Climbing Fairy

By Daisy Meadows

ORCHARD

www.rainbowmagicbooks.co.uk

The Fairyland Palace

Fairy Arena

Tippington Town

Cool Kids Leisure Centre

Jack Frost's Ice Castle

Wetherbury Village

Jack Frost's Spell

I must get strong! I'll start today.
But kids are getting in my way.
They jump and run, they spin and bound.
I can't do sports with them around!

Goblins, ruin every club.
Spoil their sports and make them blub.
I'll prove it's true, for all to see:
My sister's not as strong as me!

Contents

Chapter One
A Chilly Reception

"I can't believe that we've tried out nearly all the after-school clubs," said Kirsty Tate with a sigh.

She and her best friend Rachel Walker had already been to three taster classes. They had shared an exciting adventure in each one, because Jack Frost had stolen the four magical bracelets that belonged to the After School Sports Fairies. He wanted to shut the Cool Kids Leisure Centre down and exercise in private so that he could beat his sister Jilly Chilly at arm-wrestling. Rachel and Kirsty had promised to help get the bracelets back.

"It's been brilliant," said Rachel. "Now there's just enough time for one more try-out."

"Ready for the climbing club?" asked a voice behind them.

It was Lucy, the young woman who was organising the trial classes. She ticked off their names on her list.

"The climbing wall is through there," she said, pointing to a set of double doors. "The instructor is called Mitchell.

Have fun!"

As soon as the girls were in the climbing room, a young man bounded over to them.

"Hi, I'm Mitchell," he said. "No experience of climbing? No problem.

You can start off with bouldering, so you won't need a harness. You'll stay close to the ground."

He showed them the colour-coded paths across the wall. Rachel noticed two redheaded girls halfway up.

"Why aren't they moving?" she asked.

Mitchell frowned.

"They look scared," he said. "They told me they had climbed before. They're sisters." He cupped his hands around his mouth. "Don't panic, Amy and Fee, just make your way down slowly."

"We can't," said the bigger girl, Amy, in a shaky voice. "We're too dizzy to move."

The smaller sister, Fee, had squeezed her eyes shut.

"No worries," said Mitchell. "Freddy's right next to you. He'll give you a hand."

"Mitchell, I'm too high up," wailed the boy. "I'm afraid."

"But Freddy's been climbing for years," Mitchell murmured to himself. "I'll have to go up."

He started to pull on a harness, but the straps got tangled around his legs.

"Oops, butterfingers," he said, sitting down to free his legs. "It's lucky that those other lads aren't panicking."

There were three boys at the very top of the climbing wall. They were shoving each other and swinging on the ropes.

"Stop that, please," Mitchell called to them. "It's dangerous."

The boys sniggered, but stopped pushing each other. Mitchell stood up and put one hand on the wall.

"Wow, my head is spinning," he said in a surprised voice.

"Can we help?" asked Kirsty.

Mitchell sat down and shook his head.

"I can't climb like this," he muttered. "What's the matter with me? Have I lost my courage?"

Rachel and Kirsty exchanged a worried glance. They knew why things were going so wrong. Callie the Climbing Fairy's magical bracelet was still missing. Until it was returned, Jack Frost was going to cause trouble for climbers everywhere.

15

"The first thing is to get everyone down from the wall," said Kirsty.

An idea popped into Rachel's head. "If they can't climb down, maybe they can jump," she said. "How about a trampoline?"

"Brainwave!" exclaimed Mitchell.

They borrowed a trampoline from hall one, where Rachel and Kirsty had had their trampolining class earlier. The girls helped Mitchell to place it under the frightened climbers.

"Do you think you can jump?" Kirsty asked.

Amy and Fee smiled and nodded.

"We love trampolining," said Amy.

Soon, all three climbers were safely on the ground.

"It's funny, I didn't feel dizzy or scared when I jumped on to the trampoline," said Freddy.

"That must be because we've already got Teri the Trampolining Fairy's bracelet back," Kirsty whispered to Rachel. "It's only when they were climbing that things went wrong."

"You two have been superstars," said Mitchell. "Could you go and let Lucy know that I'm finishing the climbing class early? I don't know what's going on, but I can't run the class when I can't climb."

Rachel and Kirsty hurried back to the foyer, but Lucy wasn't there.

"Let's ask the receptionist," said Rachel.

The lady at the reception desk was wearing an electric-blue skirt suit with a matching bow at the neck, and a floppy hat that covered half her face. When the girls asked about Lucy, she didn't even look up at them.

"Lucy's not here," she snapped. "Call back tomorrow."

"I know that voice," said Kirsty.

She leaned forward and pulled the hat off. Rachel gasped when she saw the spiky hair and sharp nose.

"Jilly Chilly!" she exclaimed.

Chapter Two
Callie's Rope Trick

Jack Frost's bad-tempered little sister glared at them both.

"What are you two doing here?" she hissed. "Go away!"

"We're here to try out the after-school sports clubs," said Kirsty. "And we're also here to help our fairy friends."

Jilly Chilly narrowed her eyes.

"Do you mean that you're trying to foil my brother's plans?" she asked.

"We've already got three of the magical bracelets back," said Rachel. "And we'll get the fourth one too."

"Fine by me," said Jilly. "I hope he fails."

"You mean, you're not going to stop us?" asked Kirsty.

"Stop you?" shrieked Jilly Chilly. "No, you nincompoops. I'm going to help you!"

She jumped out from behind the desk and held her wand high above her head.

The girls shared an anxious look. They didn't like the sound of that.

"What are you thinking of doing?" Rachel asked.

"How about hitting the leisure centre with a lightning bolt?" Jilly Chilly suggested. "Or I could cover the whole place in ice."

"It's ... er ... a kind offer," said Kirsty. "But we don't want to damage the leisure centre."

"And we wouldn't want to see a sister turn against her brother," Rachel added. "It seems a bit mean."

"So what?" said Jilly Chilly. "Silly goody two-shoes. I'll find my own way to stop him."

She stamped off towards the changing rooms and the girls raced back to the climbing wall. A man was talking to Mitchell with his back to Rachel and Kirsty. He was wearing a baseball cap and a blue tracksuit.

"Bad news," said Mitchell, walking over to them. "This gentleman says that the leisure centre is closing early tonight. Would you mind tidying the climbing ropes?"

"Of course," the girls said.

Freddy, Amy and Fee were packing up

the harnesses.

"Those other boys are still climbing,"
said Rachel, looking up at the wall.
"They don't seem to be dizzy or scared."

The three boys were pulling themselves
across the wall as if it was the easiest
thing in the world. Rachel started coiling
up the first rope as she watched them.

"They're really good at climbing," she
said.

"Look down," Kirsty whispered.

Rachel looked down and forgot all
about the boys. The rope in her hand was
glowing.

"Is it magic?" she asked.

It was! The rope curved out of her
hand and slithered into a perfect circle. A
golden light flickered along it. Then the
floor inside the circle rippled like a pool,

and the tips of green fairy wings broke
through the ripples. Next moment, out
popped Callie the Climbing Fairy. She
wore colourful leggings that matched
the star on her T-shirt, and she had shiny,
short brown hair.

"Hello," she whispered. "I've come to see how your class is going."

"It's a disaster," Kirsty replied. "Almost everyone is too frightened to climb the wall, and now the leisure centre is closing early."

"It's the same in Fairyland," said Callie. "I was trying to teach climbing at the fairy school, and I was too scared to put one foot on the sparkly climbing wall. If I don't find my bracelet, how will I ever be able to help anyone again?"

"There's one odd thing," said Rachel. "Those three boys are climbing high with no fear."

As they watched, the biggest of the three boys stretched out a foot to move sideways. It was a large, bony foot – and the two girls suddenly realised why the boys were so good at climbing . . .

"They're not boys at all," said Rachel.
"They're goblins!"

Mitchell clapped his hands to get everyone's attention.

"Let's go and wait in the entrance," he said. "I want to find out what's going on. Come on down, boys."

Callie hid in Kirsty's pocket, while Rachel turned to smile at Mitchell.

"We'll follow you as soon as we've put these last ropes away," she said.

"I have to wait for the boys to come down," said Mitchell.

"I'll deal with them," said the man in the baseball cap. "You can go."

"Where have I heard that voice before?" Kirsty murmured.

She tried to look at the man's face, but he still had his back turned to them. Mitchell and the other children left the room.

"Hurry up," the man snapped at Rachel and Kirsty. "I haven't got all day."

Suddenly, Kirsty clutched Rachel's arm. "Quickly, we have to hide before he looks at us," she said in an urgent whisper. "I've just realised – that's Jack Frost in disguise!"

Chapter Three
Flopsy Popsydoodle

The girls darted behind a curtain at the far end of the room. It was a small storage space filled with boxes.

"Callie, can you turn us into fairies?" Rachel asked. "If Jack Frost sees us, he'll be on his guard."

Callie waved her rainbow-tipped wand,

and sparkling fairy dust flew into the air. As it floated down around them, the girls became as tiny as Callie, with filmy fairy wings.

"Let's go and see if we can find out anything about your missing bracelet," said Rachel, taking Callie's hand.

Together, the three fairies fluttered out from behind the curtain. They saw Jack Frost standing at the bottom of the climbing wall. He was yelling up at the goblins.

"Get down here right now, you useless lot," he roared. "You let those human children win, and now three of my bracelets are back in fairy hands. How dare you have fun while I'm still losing to Jilly Chilly?"

Rachel, Kirsty and Callie perched on top of the climbing wall as the goblins made their way down and stood in front of Jack Frost.

"I'm taking over now," Jack Frost snapped. "Give me my bracelet."

"But—" began one goblin.

Jack Frost leaned towards him, closer and closer, until the tips of their long noses met.

"Don't argue with me," hissed the Ice Lord.

The goblin shook his head and gave a high-pitched squeak. Then he dropped a gleaming bracelet into Jack Frost's hand.

"My magical bracelet!" exclaimed Callie.

Jack Frost slipped the bracelet on to his wrist and rubbed his hands together.

"Now get out of here and empty this leisure centre," he ordered. "Soon Jilly Chilly will have to admit that I am the strongest and the best."

The goblins scampered out of the room, and Jack Frost gave a chuckle.

"Now it's my turn to have some fun," he said.

He pulled himself up on to the

trampoline and started bouncing. He wasn't very good at it. He kept landing on everything except his feet. The fairies winced as he belly-flopped with a loud "OOF!"

"Goodness, he's very unfit," said Callie. "Listen to how hard he's panting after just a few bounces."

"Good workout," they heard Jack Frost mutter, gasping for breath. "I'm already ten times stronger."

"Let's try to take the bracelet off his wrist," said Kirsty. "Quickly, while he's face-down. He won't see us coming."

The three fairies swooped down and hovered around Jack Frost's outstretched arm. The bracelet seemed to glow even more brightly when Callie was nearby.

"We'll pull it off on three," Rachel whispered. "One . . . two . . ."

At that moment, the door was flung open. Rachel, Kirsty and Callie dived under the trampoline. From there, they couldn't see who had come in. They heard high heels clip-clopping over the hard floor. Then they saw a pair of feet in purple high heels with silver bows.

"How do you do," said a squeaky voice. "My name is Flopsy Popsydoodle, and I am a jewellery expert."

The fairies exchanged a confused look.

"I've just noticed your beautiful bracelet," the squeaky voice went on.

"Would you like me to tell you how much money it is worth?"

The trampoline moved as Jack Frost sat up.

"Go on," he said, jumping down to the floor. "How rich am I?"

"Take it off so I can have a closer look," the stranger said.

The fairies saw Jack Frost's curly-toed boots step up close to the purple high heels.

"Listen, Mopsywoodle, or whatever your name is," he growled, "this bracelet doesn't leave my wrist."

"Who is that?" Rachel whispered.

She fluttered closer to the edge of the trampoline.

"Be careful," said Callie with a gasp. "You could be seen."

Rachel reached the edge and tucked herself under the lip of the trampoline. She peeped through the gap where the bouncy mat was fastened to the frame.

"Oh no," she said, groaning. "It's Jilly Chilly."

Chapter Four
All Tied Up

Jilly Chilly was still in her receptionist disguise, with the large floppy hat and the big blue bow.

"Don't be silly," she snapped. "I only want to hold it for a minute."

The fairies saw Jack Frost pull his wand out of his pocket.

"Uh-oh," said Kirsty. "I think he
suspects something."

"I know who you are," he yelled. "Do
you think you can fool me? I'm too
clever and handsome to be tricked by a
silly little human."

"Pardon?" cried Jilly Chilly, her eyes
flashing with anger. "How dare you
call me a – oh – I mean – yes. I am a
human. That's right."

"You're one of those dratted children
who help the fairies," Jack Frost ranted.
"You're a pest."

Jilly Chilly turned and started to clip-
clop away.

"Oh no you don't!" Jack Frost shrieked.
He flicked his wand at the pile of
climbing ropes the girls had left. They
rose up like angry snakes, and slithered

after Jilly Chilly.

"Hey!" she yelled, as one rope wrapped itself around her ankles.

"Serves you right," Jack Frost cackled.

Another rope pinned her arms to her sides. Then Jack Frost rolled her over to lie against the climbing wall.

"Let me go!" Jilly Chilly yelled.

Jack Frost just laughed and started climbing the wall.

"I'm so clever and marvellous," he murmured to himself. "You silly humans will never take this bracelet away. I'm a genius. No one can defeat me."

"No one can stand you," hissed Jilly Chilly through gritted teeth.

"We can't just leave her lying there," said Kirsty. "But how can we rescue her right under Jack Frost's nose?"

"We have to think of a way to make him leave the room," said Rachel.

She looked around and spotted a loudspeaker on the wall.

"That's it!" she exclaimed. "All leisure centres have loudspeakers so that they can make announcements."

She beckoned Kirsty and Callie to follow her, and they fluttered up to the loudspeaker. By gently pulling at the edge, they were able to slip behind the mesh and squeeze inside.

"Callie, can you make my voice sound as if it's coming through this?" Rachel asked.

Callie waved her wand. Rachel felt a warm tickle in her throat and knew that the magic had worked.

"Could Mr Jack Frost please come to reception?" she said, trying to sound as grown-up as she could.

Her voice crackled and echoed around the room. Jack Frost twisted his head to look over his shoulder at the speaker.

"Mr Jack Frost to reception now, please," said Rachel.

Each fairy held her breath. Would he be fooled? Would he go?

Yes! He made his way down the wall with nimble grace, and glared at Jilly Chilly who was still on the ground.

"Wait there," he said. "You humans are more trouble than you're worth."

He stomped out of the room, slamming the door heavily behind him. At once, the fairies left the loudspeaker and flew over to Jilly Chilly.

"Oh, great," Jilly Chilly snarled when she saw them. "Fairies. That's all I need. Can this day get any worse?"

"Actually, we've come to make your day better," said Kirsty. "Hold still, and Callie will magic you free in a twinkle."

Callie pointed her wand at the knotted ropes, but they didn't move.

"Fat lot of good you are," Jilly Chilly grumbled.

"It must be because they're climbing ropes," said Callie. "As long as Jack Frost still has my magical bracelet, I won't be able to use any climbing magic."

"Then we'll just have to do this the old-fashioned way," said Rachel. "Callie, could you make us human again?"

With a sparkly puff of fairy dust, the girls were back to their normal size. They started to pull at the knots. Jilly Chilly's hat fell off.

"Ouch," said Kirsty. "Jack Frost's magic really tied these up well."

Callie flew to the door and let out a little cry of dismay.

"He's coming back," she exclaimed. "And he's got the goblins with him. Hurry!"

Rachel and Kirsty tugged at the knots so hard that their fingers ached.

"Come on, you pathetic humans," Jilly Chilly shouted.

"There's no need to be so rude," said Rachel. "We're trying our best."

"I think it's loosening," Kirsty cried.

But it was too late. The door burst open, sending Callie spinning through the air. Jack Frost was glaring at them from the doorway.

"What in the name of sharp, pointy icicles is going on here?" he roared.

Chapter Five
Kirsty's Competition

Rachel and Kirsty stood up and faced
Jack Frost. The goblins peeped out from
behind him, pulling faces and giggling.

"It's wrong to tie people up," said
Rachel. "We were trying to set her free."

Jack Frost looked at his prisoner. Now
that her hat had come off, it was easy to

see who she was.

"You!" he yelled. "Serves you right."

"Let me go!" Jilly Chilly screeched.

"No way," said Jack Frost. "I'm fit and strong now, after all my exercise earlier. I can easily beat you at arm-wrestling."

The girls were so astonished that they forgot to feel scared.

"What exercise are you talking about?" asked Kirsty. "You bounced on the trampoline about three times and then had to sit down for a rest."

"The only reason you would beat anyone is because you're wearing the magical bracelet," Rachel added. "You're just a big cheat."

Jack Frost's face went purple with fury.

"I don't need the bracelet to make me fit and strong," he blustered. "I just happen to like wearing it."

"Prove it," said Kirsty.

A sudden idea had darted into her mind. Everyone looked at her in surprise.

"What do you mean?" asked Callie in a whisper.

"I challenge you to a climbing competition," said Kirsty. "Take off the bracelet and compete with me fair and square. Whoever climbs highest is the winner."

"What do I get if I win?" asked Jack Frost in a suspicious voice.

"The bracelet," said Kirsty. "But if you lose, you have to give it back to Callie."

Rachel and Callie exchanged an alarmed glance.

"Kirsty, are you sure?" said Rachel.

But Callie perched on Kirsty's shoulder and gave her the

lightest of fairy kisses.

"You won't lose," she said. "All the fairies in Fairyland believe in you."

"Fine," said Jack Frost. "But let's make it even more interesting."

He swished his wand as if he were slicing through the air. There was a tremendous clap of thunder, and an icy blast of wind. Everything went dark.

"What's happening?" cried Rachel, squeezing her best friend's hand.

"I don't know," said Kirsty.

They were lifted into the air and then

dropped down on something cold and hard. They looked around and saw cliffs towering above them. Jilly Chilly was still tied up, trying to wriggle free.

"We're outside," said Kirsty in surprise.

"And we're fairies again," added Rachel, glancing over her shoulder at her gauzy wings.

The tall cliffs around them were grey, and the sky was full of storm clouds.

"I know where we are," said Callie. "These are the ice cliffs, and we're back in Fairyland."

"This is where we will have our competition," said Jack Frost.

He took off the magical bracelet and handed it to the tallest goblin. The goblin sniggered and put it on his own bony wrist.

"What about her wings?" he squawked. "Cheating fairy."

"I will fold my wings," said Kirsty in a loud voice. "I never cheat."

"Kirsty, this is a really hard climb," said

Callie in an anxious voice. "I don't want you to get hurt."

"I won't," said Kirsty. "If I fall, I'll just use my wings to fly back down. I'm more worried that I won't be able to climb high enough."

Rachel hugged her.

"You can do it," she said.

Smiling, Kirsty took her place at the foot of the cliff. Jack Frost stood beside her wearing a smug smile.

"Ready . . . " he said, "steady . . . go!"

Chapter Six
The Big Cheat

Kirsty and Jack Frost pulled themselves upwards, and everyone else started shouting.

"Jack Frost is a winner!"

"Go on, Kirsty!"

"Show that fairy who's boss!"

"Beat that stupid brother of mine!"

Kirsty went up slowly and steadily. She concentrated on moving one hand or foot at a time. It felt as if she was doing well . . . till she looked up and saw Jack Frost scrambling ahead. He was moving with speed and skill.

"There's no way I can catch up with him," said Kirsty, and her heart sank.

At the bottom of the cliff, Callie shook her head.

"Jack Frost doesn't know how to climb like that," she said. "So how is he doing it?"

Out of the corner of her eye, Rachel saw the tallest goblin fiddling with the bracelet.

"That's funny," she said. "It's not glowing like it did before."

Then she gasped, as she realised the truth.

"Callie," she whispered. "Jack Frost still has your bracelet. He gave the goblin a fake one."

Callie's eyes widened.

"What a mean thing to do," she said. "Kirsty's trying to win fair and square, but she hasn't got a chance against that cheat."

"What are we going to do?" Rachel asked.

"Set me free," said Jilly Chilly, who had been listening. "I've got an idea."

Rachel and Callie worked together to undo the tough knots. At last they

loosened, and Jilly Chilly jumped to her feet. She pulled out her wand and pointed it at her big brother.

"Hey!" she yelled. "This is for tying me up."

A spray of tiny hailstones flew from the tip of the wand. They pattered against Jack Frost's back, and then came together in the shape of a tiny tornado. It twisted down his arm and into his pocket.

"Get off!" he shouted.

Rachel, Callie and Kirsty watched in

amazement. The hailstone tornado rose
out of his pocket, and now they could see
something glowing inside it.

"My bracelet!" Callie exclaimed.

Jack Frost had gone purple with rage.
But as he was hanging on to the cliff
with both hands, he couldn't do anything.
The little tornado swirled down to the
fairies and dropped the bracelet into
Callie's hand. Then it sank into the snow
and melted away.

"Someone get me down from here!"
Jack Frost bellowed. "I can't move."

"Without the bracelet, he can't climb,"
said Callie.

Steadily, Kirsty pulled herself up beside
him.

"Put your arm around me," she said,
fluttering her wings again. "I'll help you."

Rachel flew up to Jack Frost's other side. With his arms around their shoulders, they lifted him down. As soon as he was on the ground, he started yelling at the fairies and his sister.

"You're all cheats!" he howled, jabbing his finger at them each in turn. "You — and you — and especially you!"

Jilly Chilly stuck her tongue out at him.

"There's only one cheat around here," said Callie.

"Now we can have our next arm-wrestling match," said Jilly Chilly. "Let's do it right here."

For once, Jack Frost had run out of words. He turned on his heel and stomped away. The goblins scurried after him.

Jilly Chilly threw back her head and cackled with laughter.

"That was fun," she said.

"Thank you for your help," said Callie.

But then Jilly Chilly's eyes crackled with sudden anger.

"Don't start thinking that we're friends," she hissed. "You untied me and I got your silly trinket back, so we're quits. Now leave me alone."

She whirled around and ran after her brother. The three fairies stared at each other and then burst into peals of laughter.

"Oh my goodness, that was fun, but I'm glad it's over," said Kirsty. "My heart was hammering while I climbed the cliff."

"You were super brave," said Rachel, hugging her. "Well done."

"I hope you choose to carry on with climbing," said Callie, "now that things are back to normal at the Cool Kids Leisure Centre."

"I think we should," said Rachel, and Kirsty nodded in agreement.

Callie hugged them both.

"Thank you for helping me and all the other After School Sports Fairies," she said.

"It was our pleasure," said Rachel. "Please come and see us at the climbing club any time."

"You can count on it," said Callie.

She waved her wand, and the grey mountains blurred into a mist of sparkling fairy dust. Then the two friends went whooshing through the air. Amid the sparkles, for a moment, they thought they glimpsed each of the After School Sports Fairies.

Rita the Rollerskating Fairy jumped and twirled past. Teri the Trampolining Fairy bounced up and waved. Bonnie the Bike-Riding Fairy giggled as she

wheelied along beside them, and Callie blew them a kiss. Then the sparkly mist faded, and the girls were back in the climbing room where their adventure had begun. They were human again.

"We did it!" said Kirsty.

The door opened and in came Mitchell, Freddy, Amy and Fee.

"Good news," Mitchell said when he saw the girls. "That man must have made a mistake. The leisure centre isn't closing early, and I'm feeling lots better. So I hope you're ready for that climb. Who's going first?"

The girls exchanged a happy smile.

"Definitely Kirsty," said Rachel. "I've got a feeling that she's going to be a natural!"

The End

**Now it's time for Kirsty and
Rachel to help ...**

Camilla the Christmas Present Fairy

Read on for a sneak peek ...

"Hurry up, train," said Kirsty Tate under
her breath. "I am longing to see Rachel!"

Kirsty was going to spend the week
before Christmas with her best friend
Rachel Walker in Tippington. They had
shared many adventures, and Kirsty knew
that she was going to have a wonderful
week.

Kirsty peeped into her present bag with
Christmassy excitement. It was bulging
with gifts. Her favourite one was the
friendship bracelet that she had made for
Rachel. Then she noticed that the label
had fallen off.

"Bother," she murmured.

She felt around in the bottom of the bag and pulled out a label. It said: *To Mrs Walker, love from Kirsty.*

"Oh no," said Kirsty. "All the labels have come off. I hope I can remember which present is whose."

Then she noticed a small gift wrapped in crackly gold paper.

"I don't remember wrapping that," she said.

Suddenly the gold paper started to sparkle. Twinkling silver lights flickered across it like distant stars. Could it be . . .

"Magic?" Kirsty whispered.

Ever since the day she and Rachel had met on Rainspell Island, fairy magic had been a part of their friendship. But usually their fairy friends appeared when they were together. Kirsty reached out and touched the crackly paper.

At once, a honey-coloured glow spread across the present. The gold paper curled outwards, and Kirsty saw a tiny fairy waving up at her.

Read Camilla the Christmas Present Fairy to find out what adventures are in store for Kirsty and Rachel!

Read the brand-new series from Daisy Meadows...

Ride. Dream. Believe.

Meet best friends Aisha and Emily and journey to the secret world of Unicorn Valley!

Calling all parents, carers and teachers!
The Rainbow Magic fairies are here to help
your child enter the magical world of reading.
Whatever reading stage they are at, there's
a Rainbow Magic book for everyone!
Here is Lydia the Reading Fairy's guide to
supporting your child's journey at all levels.

Starting Out

Our Rainbow Magic Beginner Readers are perfect for first-time readers who are just beginning to develop reading skills and confidence. Approved by teachers, they contain a full range of educational levelling, as well as lively full-colour illustrations.

1

Developing Readers

Rainbow Magic Early Readers contain longer stories and wider vocabulary for building stamina and growing confidence. These are adaptations of our most popular Rainbow Magic stories, specially developed for younger readers in conjunction with an Early Years reading consultant, with full-colour illustrations.

2

Going Solo

The Rainbow Magic chapter books – a mixture of series and one-off specials – contain accessible writing to encourage your child to venture into reading independently. These highly collectible and much-loved magical stories inspire a love of reading to last a lifetime.

3

www.rainbowmagicbooks.co.uk

"Rainbow Magic got my daughter reading chapter books. Great sparkly covers, cute fairies and traditional stories full of magic that she found impossible to put down" – Mother of Edie (6 years)

"Florence LOVES the Rainbow Magic books. She really enjoys reading now" – Mother of Florence (6 years)

Read along the Reading Rainbow!

Well done – you have completed the book!

This book was worth 1 star.

See how far you have climbed on the Reading Rainbow opposite.
The more books you read, the more stars you can colour in
and the closer you will be to becoming a Royal Fairy!

Do you want to print your own Reading Rainbow?

1) Go to the Rainbow Magic website

2) Download and print out the poster

3) Colour in a star for every book you finish
and climb the Reading Rainbow

4) For every step up the rainbow,
you can download your very own certificate

There's all this and lots more at
rainbowmagicbooks.co.uk

You'll find activities, stories, a special newsletter
AND you can search for the fairy with your name!